A HOMEMADE TOGETHER CHRISTMAS

PEACHTREE

MARYANN COCCA-LEFFLER

ALBERT WHITMAN & COMPANY
CHICAGO, ILLINOIS

To my mother, Rose, who taught us
that being together is the best gift of all

Love, Maryann

Library of Congress Cataloging-in-Publication data is on file with the publisher.

Text and pictures copyright © 2015 Maryann Cocca-Leffler
Published in 2015 by Albert Whitman & Company
ISBN 978-0-8075-3366-6

Printed in China
10 9 8 7 6 5 4 3 2 1 HH 20 19 18 17 16 15

Visit Maryann at www.maryanncoccaleffler.com

For more information about Albert Whitman & Company,
visit our web site at www.albertwhitman.com.

Luca was helping decorate for Christmas.

Luca's sister, Rosie, held up the star she made last year out of twigs and moss.

"The homemade ornaments are my favorite," said Momma.

"Things we make by hand are always the most special," said Dad.

"Why don't we *make* each other Christmas gifts this year?" suggested Rosie.

"We'll have a homemade Christmas!" said Momma.

"What does that mean?" asked Luca.

"We are going to make our gifts instead of buy them," explained Rosie. "I already have an idea!" She ran upstairs to her room.

"What can I make?" asked Luca.

"You'll think of something," said Dad.

Luca went to his room and
wrote some ideas in his notepad.

bake a cake

"No, I can't use the oven by myself."

plant a garden

"That won't work. It's not spring."

make a warm hat

"But I don't know how to knit."

He looked over his notes.
Luca needed some new ideas.

He followed a sweet smell to the kitchen.

"What are you doing?" Luca asked Momma.

"I'm making something for my homemade gift," said Momma.

"What is it?" asked Luca.

"You'll find out on Christmas morning!" said Momma.

"What can I make?"

"How about making something with origami?" suggested Momma.

Luca wrote in his notepad.

make paper bird

Luca tried his origami bird idea.

But he could not get the folding just right.

All that was left were mounds of paper.
So Luca wrote down some more ideas.

The next day, Luca listened at the door to Dad's workshop.

hummmmmmmmmmmmmmmmmmmmmmmmmmmmmmmmmmmmmmmmmmm

He could hear a machine humming.
"Dad! What are you doing in there?"
yelled Luca.

"Don't come in! I'm working on my gift!"
called Dad.

"What is it?" Luca asked.

"You'll see on Christmas morning,"
said Dad.

"What can I make?"

"How about making something to eat?"
suggested Dad.

Luca wrote in
his notepad.

make
honey
granola

Luca tried his honey granola idea.
But Luca loved honey more than anything.

All that was left was a big, empty jar and a giant bellyache.

Luca heard music coming
from Rosie's room.
He knocked on the wall.
"Rosie! What are you
doing in there?" he yelled.

"I'm working on my gift," Rosie said.

"What is it?" Luca asked.

"You'll find out on Christmas morning," Rosie said.

"What can I make?"

"How about building something out of snow?" suggested Rosie.

Luca wrote in his notepad.

Luca tried his snow bear idea.

build a
snow bear

But the sun got a little too warm for a snow bear.

All that was left was a long wet scarf.

On Christmas Eve everyone was
busy putting the finishing touches
on their gifts.

Luca was worried. He still did not have an
idea for his Christmas gift.

Momma peeked into Luca's room.

"Momma, I have no gift to give," said Luca.

"You know, Luca," said Momma gently, "the best part of Christmas is spending time together. There is no better gift." She gave Luca a big hug and a kiss good night.

Luca thought about what Momma had said. He looked around his room at the red scarf, the empty jar, and the mounds of paper, and finally got a great idea. He jumped out of bed and went right to work.

Luca was so excited that he woke everyone before sunrise. "Merry Christmas!"

He proudly presented his homemade gift. "In this jar are 365 days of Together To-Dos. We start today!"

Luca turned to Rosie. "Pick one."

Rosie dug her hand deep inside the jar and pulled out their very first Together To-Do.

watch the sunrise from the porch

"That's perfect!"

Momma said, and held up her homemade gift.

"We can have breakfast on the porch!"

"That's perfect!" said Dad, pulling out his homemade gift. "We'll need this!"

"Let's go!" said Rosie. "I can give everyone my gift outside."

Together they ate the delicious homemade Christmas-tree pancake.

Together they snuggled under the homemade blanket for four.

Together they listened to Rosie sing her homemade Christmas song.

Together they watched the sun peek over the mountain, slowly lighting up the field.

"Merry Homemade Christmas!" said Momma.

"And a Happy Together Year!" said Luca.